CAVE HILL TREASURE
TREASURE
And
OTHER STORIES

The Fairfield Friends Devotional Adventures

Firecracker Power and Other Stories
The Lightning Escape and Other Stories
Blaze on Rocky Ridge and Other Stories
Cave Hill Treasure and Other Stories

9801

NANCY SPECK

A FAIRFIELD FRIENDS DEVOTIONAL ADVENTURE

CAVE HILL TREASURE

And
OTHER STORIES

BETHANY HOUSE PUBLISHERS
MINNEAPOLIS, MINNESOTA 55438

Published by Bethany House Publishers
A Ministry of Bethany Fellowship International
11300 Hampshire Avenue South
Minneapolis, Minnesota 55438

Printed in the United States of America by
Bethany Press International, Minneapolis, Minnesota 55438

Library of Congress Cataloging-in-Publication Data

Speck, Nancy.
    Cave Hill treasure and other stories with take-away value / by
Nancy Speck.
        p.   cm. — (A Fairfield Friends devotional adventure)
        Summary: A group of friends make some important discoveries
about respect, revenge, faithfulness and other Christian values. Each
episode is followed by questions and suggested Bible verses.
        ISBN 0–7642–2007–1 (pbk.)
        [1. Christian life—Fiction. 2. Conduct of life—Fiction.] I. Title.
II. Series: Speck, Nancy. Fairfield Friends devotional adventure.
PZ7.S7412Cav   1998
[Fic]—dc21   97–45449
                                                                         CIP
                                                                          AC

For R.V.G.
Thanks for baby-sitting.

NANCY SPECK is a free-lance writer and home-maker who has published numerous articles, stories, and poems. Her background in creative writing and social work gives her unique insight into the importance and challenge of teaching children Christian character traits at an early age. Nancy and her husband, Brian, have two elementary-age daughters and make their home in Pennsylvania.

Contents

The Fairfield Friends

Cameron Parker

Cameron is very smart in math and science and is in third grade at a private school, Foster Academy. He lives with his parents, older brother, Philip, and younger sister, Justine.

Ceely Coleman

Ceely, short for Cecilia, is hardworking and serious. She is in fourth grade at Morgandale Christian School, plays field hockey, and has a black cat named Snowball.

Hutch Coleman

Hutch, short for Hutchinson, is Ceely's younger brother. He's a second grader at Morgandale Christian School and is the class clown.

# of Fairfield Court

Min Hing

Min, a third-grade student at Fairfield Elementary, lives with her parents and grandmother. She's quiet and shy, takes ballet lessons, and plays the piano.

Valerie Stevens

Valerie lives with her mother and little sister, Bonnie, since her parents are divorced. Valerie, who is friendly and outspoken, is an average student in second grade at Fairfield Elementary.

Roberto Ruiz

Roberto, a fourth grader at Fairfield Elementary, has lived with his grandpop ever since his parents died. His older brother, Ramone, lives with them. Roberto plays soccer and has a dog named Freckles.

1

The Disappearing Shoes

G o, Ceely!" screamed Valerie at the top of her lungs.

Ceely's head turned toward the bleachers. She waved at Valerie, Roberto, Min, Hutch, and Cameron, her friends from the Fairfield Court neighborhood.

"Beat Creekview!" Valerie continued.

Hutch put his hands over his ears. "I think you broke my eardrums," he said as he turned to Valerie.

Valerie giggled. "Sorry, Hutch," she said. "I just want Morgandale Christian School to win their first field hockey game, especially since it's against Creekview Elementary."

"Same here," responded Roberto. "The kids at Creekview always brag about how good their sports teams are."

A whistle blew and the game began. The five friends watched as Ceely hit the field hockey ball down the field. Suddenly, she tripped. Ceely sprawled onto the ground.

"Did you see that?" exclaimed Cameron.

"That girl hit Ceely's leg on purpose," added Hutch.

The Fairfield Friends watched as Creekview and Morgandale Christian battled for the ball. Each time Ceely or her teammates controlled the ball, the other team slyly swatted one of them, pushed them, or tripped them. Even though Coach Hardy pointed out this roughness to the referee, she said that it was just part of the game.

During the second half, Roberto's soccer buddies, Brad, Tony, and Josh, joined the Fairfield Friends.

"I didn't think girls got so nasty," Brad remarked as he watched a player whack Ceely on the ankle.

"If someone did that to me," said Tony, "I'd smack them back."

It wasn't long before Creekview scored. They scored again just before the final whistle ended the game.

"You played really well," Min said to Ceely as she joined them after the game.

"Yeah," agreed Cameron. "You made some nice hits."

"Oh, cut the sweetness," said Brad. "If Creekview hadn't done all that rough playing, Ceely's team would have won."

"I'd like to teach them a lesson," said Josh.

"Me too," Roberto said.

"Maybe we can get back at them," suggested Tony, "by doing something to their soccer team. Fairfield Elementary plays Creekview next week."

"That would be great," said Hutch.

"Hutch!" said Ceely. "What are you saying?" She turned to her friends. "The other team was pretty mean to us," said Ceely. "But doing something to get even with them makes us just as wrong. At chapel today, the speaker talked about not seeking revenge. He quoted Romans 12:19, which says, 'Do not try to punish others when they wrong you. Wait for God to punish them with his anger.' "

"Oh yeah," said Hutch weakly. "I forgot."

"I guess you're right," said Roberto.

Brad, Tony, and Josh rolled their eyes at one another and snickered.

————

The following Tuesday, the Fairfield Friends

met again after school to watch Roberto's soccer game. While they waited, they suddenly heard the fire alarm go off in the school. Both soccer teams filed out a side door to the playground.

"Why would they have a fire drill after school?" asked Valerie.

"Maybe it's a real fire," said Min.

"But there aren't any fire trucks coming," Ceely added.

Cameron and Hutch looked at the others and shrugged. Five minutes later, the teams returned to the locker room. But it was another fifteen minutes before the teams came to the field. And when they did, the Creekview team was in bare feet!

The coach met with the referee, who then turned to the crowd.

"Creekview Elementary is unable to play today's game. During the fire alarm, all their soccer shoes and sneakers disappeared. The alarm was set off by someone other than the principal to provide the time needed to take the shoes. School employees are searching for the shoes and talking to anyone who was in the school at the time."

A few minutes later, Roberto joined the rest of his friends. As they discussed what had happened, Ceely suddenly interrupted.

"Look at those three," she said, pointing to Roberto's three soccer pals. They were walking toward the bleachers, laughing and slapping one another on the back. "I'll bet they had something to do with this."

"I thought the same thing," Roberto agreed. "They didn't act surprised at all when the coach told us what happened."

"But how could they have done anything?" Cameron asked. "Weren't they all with you when the fire alarm went off?"

Roberto thought for a minute, then frowned. "Josh and Tony came out, but I don't remember seeing Brad outside."

"I'll bet Brad set off the alarm," said Min.

"And while everyone was outside, he grabbed the shoes and put them somewhere," finished Valerie.

"You're right," said Hutch. "And without their shoes, Creekview wouldn't be able to play. They'd have to take a loss for the game."

"Revenge completed," said Ceely. "This is a payback to Creekview for the field hockey game."

The Fairfield Friends looked at one another and sighed. They were sure that Brad, Tony, and Josh had hidden the shoes.

"But where could they hide all those shoes?" asked Cameron.

"Yeah," Min added. "People have been looking for them, but no one's found them."

Just as Min finished, they watched Brad, Tony, and Josh round the corner of the bleachers and disappear underneath. Roberto whispered to Valerie. Then he quietly spoke to the others.

Valerie slowly slid her way along the wooden seats of the bleachers. Near the other end, she stopped. Valerie leaned forward, turning her ear toward the space a couple seats in front of her. After a few minutes, Valerie smiled. Then she quietly slipped back to the others.

"You were right, Roberto," she said. "They were bragging about taking the shoes. Brad hid them in the equipment room in a big bag of basketballs. He stuck them on the bottom so if anyone looked, all they'd see were the balls."

"OK," said Roberto. "I've got a plan. All of you go down and talk to them. Keep them busy while I go to the locker room."

Five minutes later, Roberto returned. As he joined the others, an uproar sounded from the door of the locker room. Several school teach-

ers hurried toward the soccer field, their arms full of soccer shoes.

"How'd they find the shoes?" demanded Brad, his face scrunched in anger.

Roberto shrugged and then hurried onto the playing field.

Both teams played hard, kicking and passing the ball up and down the field. At half time, the score was 1–1. When the second half started, the Creekview players got rougher. One pushed Roberto down as he kicked the ball.

Suddenly, Brad ran up to the player who'd

pushed Roberto and shoved him to the ground. Josh and Tony joined in, as well as two other Creekview players. The referee removed all six players from the game. Both teams put in substitutes, and the game continued. When the game ended, Fairfield Elementary had beaten Creekview 3–2.

After the game, the Fairfield Friends all walked home together, laughing and talking about the game.

"It's a good thing you told someone where the shoes were in time to play the game," said Valerie.

"But I didn't tell anybody where the shoes were," Roberto answered.

The others stopped and stared at him.

Roberto continued. "If I had told, Brad, Josh, and Tony would have done something to pay me back for getting them in trouble. I figured I'd leave their punishment up to God. So when I went to the equipment room, I opened up the basketball bag. When no one was around, I dumped the balls all over the locker room. I left then, but I knew when someone put the balls back, they'd find the shoes."

The friends whooped loudly. After slapping some high fives with Roberto, they slowly strolled the rest of the way to Fairfield Court.

Things to Think About

Why did the Fairfield Friends want to get even with the Creekview team? Why did they change their minds?

_____

_____

_____

How did the friends keep Roberto's buddies from "paying back" the Creekview team?

_____

_____

_____

How did God show His control of the situation and His punishment of the disobedient players?

_____

_____

Read 1 Peter 3:8–9 and 1 Thessalonians 5:15. How are you to act when someone does something wrong to you?

_____

_____

_____

Read Romans 12:17–19. Who is responsible for punishment of others' wrongdoing?

_____

_____

Read Psalm 34:15–22; 103:6; and Proverbs 20:22. What does God promise you when you are hurt or wronged by another?

_____

_____

Let's Act It Out!

Memorize Romans 12:19.

Solve the code for an important message.
Hint:
    C=A, D=B, E=C
Rcwkpi dcem c ytqpi hqp c ytqpi ukorna
ocigu aqw ytqpi.
The answer is on page 127.

Learn the "Peanut Butter and Jelly Rules of Wrongdoing."
For lunch this week make a peanut butter and jelly sandwich to help you remember each truth.

P—*Pray* for strength to avoid punishing someone who acts wrongly toward you.

B—Ask God to *Bless* the wrongdoer and show him his hurtful ways.

J—Remember that God is fair and *Just* and will bring His *Judgment* on the wrongdoer.

2

Our Boat Is Sinking!

F or the last time, Carl, sit down!" said Min's teacher Mrs. Stake.

"Are you gonna make me?" Carl shot back, a smirk on his face.

Mrs. Stake quickly called the office on her room phone. A few minutes later, Principal Martin removed Carl from the class.

I can't believe anyone could be so disrespectful, thought Min.

On the way home after school, Min told Roberto and Valerie all about the problem with Carl McMullen.

"I'd never talk back like that," Valerie said when she'd finished.

"I can believe it, though," said Roberto. "His sister Megan is in my class, and she's just as disrespectful."

The friends continued on for a couple more blocks. Then Valerie turned down her street. She told Min and Roberto that she'd meet them shortly at the Community Recreation Center, where they planned to go swimming.

After another block, Min and Roberto parted at Min's house. But ten minutes later, Roberto arrived back at the Hings'. Grandmother asked Roberto to come in while Min finished stuffing a towel in her pool bag.

"I hope you are a good swimmer, Roberto," said Grandmother.

Before he could answer, Min blurted out, "Of course he is, Grandmother. He's not scared of the water like you are."

Grandmother, concern showing on her face, continued. "Will there be a lifeguard on duty the whole time?"

Min sighed and rolled her eyes at Roberto. "Yeesss, Grandmother, there's always a guard on duty."

"Well, just be careful. The water can be dangerous."

Without another word, not even a good-bye, Min grabbed her bag and headed out the door. Roberto said good-bye to Grandmother Hing and followed Min.

"Boy," said Roberto to Min as they started

up the street. "You sure weren't very nice to your grandmother."

"Huh?" asked Min.

"You said some pretty unkind things, and you spoke to her in a . . . well . . . nasty way."

Min shrugged. "She's always bugging me about stuff, and she's so old-fashioned. Every time I go swimming, she thinks I'm going to drown or something. Besides, she's not Mother or Father or Mrs. Stake. She's just my grandmother."

"But, Min," continued Roberto, "the Bible says, 'Show respect to old people.' That's the first part of Leviticus 19:32. My grandpop made me memorize it. He always reminds me that I must respect him and everyone else."

"Boy, Roberto," Min responded. "You make me sound like Carl McMullen."

Roberto looked at her but said nothing more.

When Min returned home from swimming, she dumped her swim bag on the floor of her bedroom. Then she hurried downstairs to set the table for dinner.

While the Hing family ate, Min's father asked her about her day. She told him she'd gone swimming at the rec center with Valerie and Roberto.

"By the way, Min," said Grandmother, "you left your wet suit and towel in the bag."

"Min!" exclaimed her mother. "How many times must you be told to hang up your suit and towel after swimming? Wet things get mildew on them."

"Sorry," Min mumbled. She excused herself from the table and went to empty her bag. When she returned, she yanked out her chair and flopped down.

Min's father frowned at her. "Watch your attitude," he warned.

Min silently played with her beans. Then she burst out, "Why were you sneaking around in my room?" she demanded, staring angrily at Grandmother.

"Min!" exclaimed her father. "You will leave the table this minute."

As Min stood up, she continued. "But Grandmother is always picking on me and embarrassing me in front of my friends."

"You will be grounded for a week. Except for school, piano lessons, and ballet class, you won't be permitted out of your room. I don't want to hear anything else from you except an apology to your grandmother."

Min muttered a "sorry" and quickly left the dining room.

After school the next day, Min was just finishing her homework when the doorbell rang. Since it was time to set the table, Min walked downstairs.

"Who's that?" she asked her mother on her way to the kitchen.

"A reporter from the *Morgandale Daily Sentinel*," her mother answered. "The paper is interviewing Grandmother for an article about the interesting lives of the elderly who live in Morgandale."

Grandmother's life . . . interesting? thought Min. *I know she came to the United States when Father was a little boy. And I think Father's father died on the way or something. But why would that be interesting?* Min wondered.

A few days later, the article appeared in the paper, along with a picture of Grandmother and some other senior citizens in Morgandale. But Min had too much homework and other things to do to take time to read the story.

At school the following day, Valerie and Roberto ran up to Min when she arrived.

"That is so cool about your grandmother," said Valerie.

"You never told us anything about her journey to America," Roberto added.

Min just stared at them, not knowing what to say.

All during the school day, kids and teachers stopped Min to talk to her about her grandmother. And each time Min felt more embarrassed for not knowing any of the story about her grandmother. But the final blow came at the end of the day. Just as she was leaving the classroom, Mrs. Stake stopped her.

"Min, if it would be all right with you, I'd like you to give a little talk tomorrow about your grandmother. I think everybody read the article in the paper, but you could add so much more information. I think your classmates would enjoy it."

Min managed to nod her head in agreement.

At home, Min decided she had better study the article about her grandmother. She stretched out on her bed with the paper and began to read.

> *Another senior member of our community is Mrs. Soon Lee Hing. Mrs. Hing came to the United States almost forty years ago with her infant son, with whom she now lives. She*

shared her incredible story with me.

Min paused while she turned the page. Then she began reading her grandmother's words.

"My husband and I, our three-month-old son, and many other villagers wanted to come to America for a better life. We found a boat that was sailing to the United States, and many people crowded onto it. Too many. Somehow we stayed afloat. But when we came in sight of the American shore, people

began shouting, 'Our boat is sinking, our boat is sinking!'

"I clutched my son tightly and found myself struggling in the water. Luckily, I could swim. My husband and most of the others could not and drowned within minutes. Then I saw two children. They had grabbed on to a small piece of wood from the boat, but it wasn't big enough to keep them both afloat. Somehow, I got to them. With God's strength, I kept them, my son, and myself alive until a rescue boat came."

The newspaper words began to blur. Min continued to read about how her grandmother stayed with the children. She cared for them as if they were her own until they were adopted into good homes.

Min dropped the paper and buried her face in her pillow. *What a dope I've been*, she thought as tears dampened her bedspread. *No wonder Grandmother gets worried when I go swimming.*

Half an hour later, Min found Grandmother and apologized properly for her disrespect. She held the newspaper up. "I never knew any of this," she said sadly.

"Well, Min," answered Grandmother. "You never seemed interested, so I didn't want to bore you with it."

"Would you tell me about it now?"

Grandmother smiled. "I'll do better than that."

She went to her room, and when she returned, she had a photo album with her. Grandmother showed her pictures of Min's grandfather and her father when he was a baby. She pointed out the two children she saved. And she told Min all about her life.

The next day, Min was more than prepared for her talk in class. But she decided that telling her classmates about Grandmother wasn't enough. Instead, she took Grandmother to school so they could meet her themselves.

Things to Think About

How was Min disrespectful to her grandmother?

_____

_____

What did Min learn about her grandmother?

_____

_____

How did Min change toward her grandmother?

_____

_____

Read 1 Thessalonians 5:12–13 and Leviticus
18:4. Why should you respect others?

_____

_____

_____

Read Leviticus 19:3, 32 and 1 Peter 2:17. Who
should you show respect to?

_____

_____

_____

Read Exodus 20:12 and Proverbs 13:13. What are the benefits of being respectful?

_____

_____

Let's Act It Out!

Memorize Leviticus 19:32.

Get to know the elderly members in your church. Learn to respect them for the lives they've led and the experiences they've had. Perhaps your youth group or Sunday school class could make a schedule to visit them on a regular basis. Or plan a Saturday Servant Day in which you go to older members' homes to do some chores for them like cleaning or raking leaves.

Make a list of ways that people show disrespect for the elderly. Now list ways that you can show respect to older folks.

3

Sheep and Wolves

Rachel's here!" yelled Mr. Coleman up the steps.

Within seconds, Ceely and Hutch thundered down the stairs to greet their baby-sitter. Rachel Boardman had been their baby-sitter since they were babies. Even though she was in college now, she still baby-sat sometimes for the Colemans. They were always excited to see her.

As soon as Mr. and Mrs. Coleman left, Ceely and Hutch eagerly told Rachel about all they'd been doing at school and with the Fairfield Friends. Later on, they had some ice cream. While they ate, the doorbell rang.

Rachel stood up. "I'll see who it is," she said. "You guys finish your ice cream before it melts."

A few minutes later, she walked into the kitchen with another girl. "Ceely, Hutch, this is Connie Post. She's in my history class at college."

"Hi," said Connie.

Ceely and Hutch returned the greeting.

"Connie's been going house to house to hand out a flier about a fund-raiser tomorrow." She showed them the paper Connie had given her, then laid it on the table. "Hope for Tomorrow, a new church group on campus, is having a car wash, bake sale, and flower sale at the college gym. The money earned will be used to buy sheets, towels, and blankets for Safe Harbor and food for the Morgandale Food Bank."

"Safe Harbor!" said Ceely excitedly.

"Fairfield Court always takes canned food to the homeless shelter at Christmas," Hutch said.

"I know," said Rachel smiling. "That's why I thought you'd like to come with me tomorrow to help at the car wash."

"We sure could use the help," said Connie.

"We'll have to ask our parents," Ceely replied.

"I'll ask them when they get home," offered Rachel.

"Great," said Hutch. "Thanks."

While Rachel walked Connie back to the front door, Ceely picked up the paper Connie had given Rachel. *Hope for Tomorrow*, read Ceely. Underneath the name she read, *To have hope for tomorrow, you must trust in yourself today*.

Ceely frowned and showed it to Hutch.

Hutch shrugged. "So what?"

"That doesn't sound right," she said. "We're supposed to trust in God."

"But it says here about working for God," he said.

Before Hutch and Ceely could discuss it further, Rachel returned to the kitchen and announced it was time for bed. While they rinsed their bowls, Rachel wiped off the table. As she did, she picked up the paper Connie had given her and stuffed it in the trash can.

————

The next morning, Ceely and Hutch cheered when they found out their parents said they could help at the car wash.

"Rachel seems to be informed about the group," said Mr. Coleman.

"And we know you'll be safe with her," added Mrs. Coleman.

At 9:00 Rachel picked up Ceely and Hutch and drove to the college. They found Connie, who introduced them to Sam Brisker and Betty Clark, the student leaders of Hope for Tomorrow. After filling buckets with soapy water, they waited for dirty cars to pull into the parking lot.

During the next two hours, the group washed twenty cars. Other members of the group sold food, roses, and plants to people. During a slow period around lunch, Sam brought his car over to be washed.

"His car has so much rust and chipped

paint," Hutch said as he wiped a sponge over the hood. "Washing it isn't going to help much."

"Yeah," agreed Ceely. "It's in awful shape."

"Hey!" shouted Hutch suddenly. "There's Roberto's brother, Ramone, and his friend Ross."

Ceely and Hutch waved as their truck stopped behind Sam's.

"What are you two doing here?" asked Ramone after rolling down the window.

Ceely and Hutch explained how they learned about the group and that they needed help to raise money for Safe Harbor.

"Yeah, we know about their fund-raisers," said Ross. He reached onto the dashboard for a paper. "These were put on car windshields all over campus."

Ceely and Hutch looked at each other.

"Connie gave us that same paper when she stopped at the house last night," Ceely said.

"After reading it," Ramone continued, "we decided to come over and check out the group. Some of the things they say on the flier aren't quite right."

"See," said Ceely to Hutch. "I told you the part about trusting in yourself was wrong."

"You're absolutely right," said Ramone.

"But there is a bunch more that's wrong. It says here that your good works for the needy will help you work your way to heaven."

"Helping others is great," explained Ross. "But no one can work their way to heaven by doing a certain number of good deeds. Heaven is a gift from God to those who believe in Him by faith and obey Him."

"Hi, Ross. Hi, Ramone," said a voice suddenly. It was Rachel. "What's up? You guys need your truck washed?"

Ramone, Ross, Ceely, and Hutch turned to Rachel and told her about their concerns regarding the group.

"Wow," said Rachel when they'd finished. "I just figured since Connie said it was a religious group that it was a good group. The flier must have fooled her, too."

"But they're going to give the money earned to Safe Harbor," Hutch protested.

"Well, maybe," answered Rachel. "But I don't think we should continue to help until we find out more about them."

After returning to the Colemans' house, Rachel explained to Ceely and Hutch's parents what they'd found out about the group. "I'm sorry I didn't pay more attention to the flier," Rachel apologized. "I would have realized they weren't what they claimed to be."

"Jesus warns us in Matthew 24:11," Mr. Coleman replied, "that 'many false prophets will come and cause many people to believe false things.' Matthew 7:15 says that they trick us by pretending to be gentle lambs when they are actually sneaky, ferocious wolves." He smiled at Rachel. "You did the right thing by coming home and telling us."

That evening, the Coleman family ate at their favorite restaurant, Uncle Elmo's Burger Barn. While they were stopped at a traffic light on the way home, a small sports car raced through the intersection.

"Hey!" yelled Hutch. "That was Sam and Betty in that car."

"But they had that old clunker this morning," Ceely said. "How could they afford an expensive car like that?" she asked.

Suddenly, they looked at each other, their eyes open wide.

Their dad peered at them in his rearview mirror. "I think we all know the answer to that. And I think I'd better make a call to the college to check this group out."

"It might be a good idea to see if any of the fund-raiser money actually went to Safe Harbor or the food bank," Mom suggested.

"Or if they used all of it to help them buy a new car," finished Hutch glumly.

———

The next week, Mr. Coleman called the directors of Safe Harbor and the local food bank. Neither had received any money from Hope for Tomorrow.

On Friday, Mr. Coleman arranged some time off from work. He picked up Ceely and Hutch at school and drove to Morgandale Community College. In the parking lot of one of the buildings, Rachel, Ross, and Ramone met them.

"Thanks for coming along," said Mr. Coleman. "I think all of you are needed to tell the college officials about this group."

They met with Mrs. Young, who was in charge of student activities. She entered Hope for Tomorrow into the computer. The computer printout stated no group by that name had registered with the college.

"I wonder . . ." said Mrs. Young. She typed in Betty Clark and Sam Brisker. She laughed sadly at what she saw on the screen. "Neither of them is even a student here." She turned to the group. "I'll notify the college security guards about them. Thanks for your help," she finished.

The group walked slowly out of the building. "I'm sure glad we caught that set of wolves," said Ceely.

The others agreed.

Things to Think About

What did Ceely think about Hope for Tomorrow's flier?

Why did Ceely, Hutch, and Rachel volunteer to help with the car wash? What made them decide to leave?

What made Mr. Coleman decide to contact the college about Hope for Tomorrow?

Read 2 Peter 2:1. What is a false prophet or false teacher?

Read Matthew 7:15; Mark 13:22; and Colossians 2:8. How do false prophets trick people into believing them?

Read Ephesians 2:8–9. What is the only way that someone is "saved" for heaven?

_____

_____

Let's Act It Out!

Memorize Matthew 24:11.

Explain or write down what the following verse means: "They come to you and look gentle like sheep. But they are really dangerous like wolves" (Matthew 7:15).

_____

_____

Do this craft and role play exercise to help you understand that how false teachers look on the outside is not what they are like on the inside. Make a mask of a gentle animal or pleasant, smiling person. Using a paper plate, staple or tape a piece of string or yarn to each side so it fits snugly on the head. With an adult's help, cut out eyes with a scissors. Now make a nose and mouth and hair with markers, crayons, and yarn. First act out the part of the mask (lamb, kitten, puppy, smiling person). Then take off the mask and act like who you are really pretending to be (fox, lion, wolf, mean person).

Hanging by a Rope

Oh no!" Valerie yelled. "Look!" She pointed to the TV screen.

Valerie and Cameron were watching a video about a family on a camping trip. While on a hike, a couple of the kids had found a rope-and-board bridge hanging over a deep gully with a river roaring below. Although a sign said "Do Not Run or Jump on Bridge," the two kids were jumping up and down on it. An older sister, standing on the bank, yelled at them to get off. But the kids wouldn't listen to her.

"Why doesn't the sister go tell her parents?" Cameron asked. "She knows that jumping on the bridge is dangerous."

Suddenly, the camera zoomed in on the worn and rotted rope connecting the bridge to the other side. It began to pull apart.

47

"Get off!" hollered Cameron. "It's going to snap!"

The kids in the video, finally realizing what was happening, started to run. Just before they reached the ledge, the bridge broke away on the other side. The kids grabbed on to the wooden planks, screaming. The older sister ran for their parents. Luckily the father reached the bridge and was able to haul them up before they slipped off.

"Wow!" exclaimed Valerie. "That was an exciting movie."

"Sure was," Cameron agreed.

"Is your movie finished?" asked Mrs. Parker as she walked into the family room.

"Yeah, Mom," answered Cameron as he hit the rewind button on the VCR.

"Then after a snack, you two get ready for bed." She turned to Valerie. "I think Bonnie is finally asleep. I left the night-light on so you can see when you get into bed."

"OK," said Valerie. "Thank you."

Valerie and her little sister were spending the weekend with the Parkers. Mrs. Stevens' sister was in the hospital for an operation, and Mrs. Stevens wanted to visit her. But since her sister lived four hours away, she had arranged for Valerie and Bonnie to stay with the Parkers.

Cameron's family had a guest room with two extra beds.

———

The next morning, after everyone had finished breakfast, Mr. Parker told everyone to get in the van. They were driving to the state capital to spend the day at the Scientific Discovery Museum.

"Cool," said Valerie. "I've never been there."

"It's great," Cameron said. "It has all these experiments that kids can do."

An hour later, the Parker family, Bonnie, and Valerie entered the science center. Bonnie stayed with Mr. and Mrs. Parker. But Cameron and Valerie, along with Cameron's sister and brother, Justine and Philip, visited each display on their own.

"Look at this!" said Cameron as he moved among a bunch of kids.

"Awesome!" exclaimed Valerie when she caught up with him.

They looked in wonder at a plastic beach ball that floated in mid-air over an air vent. Suddenly, two kids ran up to look at the ball.

"I was here first," yelled a girl with a ponytail as her brother pushed her out of his way. "I'm telling Dad."

"Oh brother," said Philip, shaking his head. "What a tattletale."

"Let's go over there," suggested Cameron, pointing across the room.

They entered a room that had light shining through an opening onto a blank wall. The four of them stuck their hands into the beam of light to make shadow pictures on the wall.

Two boys walked in and stood next to Valerie and Cameron. After making shadows a few minutes, the one boy spoke. "Hey, Tyler," he said. "I'm bored with shadows. Let's go see something else."

"No way," Tyler answered back. "This is cool. I'm staying here."

"But we're supposed to stay together, and I want to go," said his brother. "I'm gonna tell Mom you won't stay with me."

"Don't you tattle on me again, Jeff. You've been ratting on me all day." He raced out of the room after Tyler.

Cameron and Valerie told Justine and Philip about the tattling boys as they left the room. After visiting the rest of the exhibits, they joined Mr. and Mrs. Parker and Bonnie.

On their way home, the group stopped for

lunch. While they waited for their food, they all noticed a family at a nearby table. Three kids were picking on one another and taking one anothers' napkins. They kicked one another under the table. Each one in turn tattled on another.

"They sound like some kids we heard at the science center," said Cameron.

"Yeah," Valerie agreed. "These kids kept tattling on one another."

Mr. and Mrs. Parker said that they'd overheard similar squabbling and tattling while they toured the center.

"Did you know there's a Bible verse about tattling?" Dad asked them.

"You're kidding, right?" said Philip.

"James 5:9," began Mr. Parker. " 'Brothers, do not complain against each other. If you do not stop complaining, you will be judged guilty.' The verse might not use the exact word 'tattling,' " Mr. Parker explained, "but complaining against one another is what tattling is. Of course, if someone is doing something dangerous or destructive, their behavior should be reported. But most tattling is done just to get the other person in trouble for no good reason."

Later that day, while waiting for dinner to

be ready, Cameron and Valerie decided to take a walk around the neighborhood. They strolled down Juniper Street and turned onto Hillside Drive. Up ahead, they saw some kids skate-boarding in their driveway.

"That's Brian and Jesse Carpenter, isn't it?" asked Cameron.

"Yeah," answered Valerie.

"Brian can do some great tricks on his board," Cameron said as he watched Brian jump up and down from the skateboard.

"What's that big truck parked at the next house?" asked Valerie.

"Looks like a moving truck," Cameron answered.

All at once a car appeared from behind the truck.

"Wow!" exclaimed Cameron. "I never saw that car at all. It was hidden by the truck."

"Well, if we can't see cars coming, Brian and Jesse can't, either. The truck blocks their view of the street at the end of their driveway."

"And that means cars can't see Brian and Jesse," concluded Cameron. "C'mon. We better warn them."

They ran down the street and up the driveway. But after showing them the danger, Brian and Jesse just laughed and told them to leave them alone.

As they started walking away, Cameron turned to Valerie. "Maybe we should tell their parents."

"I don't want to tattle on them," said Valerie.

"But this is dangerous," argued Cameron.

Valerie was silent for a moment. Then her eyes opened wide. "It's just like the movie we saw," she exclaimed. "We know what could happen, just like the sister knew at the bridge with the rotten ropes."

Cameron and Valerie ran around the back of the house to the patio door. Jesse and Brian's grandparents, who were baby-sitting, answered the door. After Cameron and Valerie explained the dangerous situation out front, they all ran through the house and out the front door.

"Brian, Jesse, no more skateboarding down the driveway. It's too dangerous right now with the truck parked there."

"Aww," said Brian. He picked up his board and walked slowly up the driveway. "Tattle-tales," he said quietly as he passed Cameron and Valerie.

Just then Brian tripped over a crack in the driveway. His skateboard flew out of his hand and rolled down the driveway and into the street.

Screech! Bang! CRACK! A car slowly appeared from behind the truck. The skateboard lay smashed flat in the street, pieces of splintered wood everywhere.

Jesse and Brian, their grandparents, Valerie, and Cameron all looked at one another. Their silence said they all realized what could have just happened.

A short time later, after the driver apologized and the skateboard was cleaned up, Valerie and Cameron hurried home. They were hungry, and they couldn't wait to watch another exciting video that evening.

Things to Think About

What things did the Parkers overhear at the science center and in the restaurant?

_____

_____

Why did Cameron and Valerie decide to report Brian and Jesse's activities?

_____

_____

What happened to Brian's skateboard? What could have happened to him?

_____

_____

Read Proverbs 10:19 and James 5:9. Why do you need to control yourself from tattling?

_____

_____

Read Proverbs 3:30. List some wrong reasons for reporting someone's actions. What are some good reasons to report another's behavior?

_____

_____

Read James 3:5–6. How is a tattling tongue like a forest fire?

_____

_____

Let's Act It Out!

Memorize James 5:9.

Read the situations below. If reporting the behavior would be tattling, put a T on the line. If it is dangerous, destructive, or damaging behavior that should be reported, put a D on the line.

_____ 1. Your sister practiced the piano for twenty-five minutes instead of thirty.

_____ 2. You find your next door neighbors behind their house playing with matches.

_____ 3. A classmate ran in front of you on the playground and took the last swing.

_____ 4. Your brother turned on the TV after your parents said not to.

_____ 5. A classmate called you hurtful names at recess.

_____ 6. Your little brother is sitting behind the couch plugging and unplugging a lamp cord in an electrical outlet.

_____ 7. The kids down the street brag to you about throwing rocks at the basement windows of several houses and breaking one of them.

_____ 8. Your sister keeps pulling the cat's tail.

_____ 9. When returning to your seat after turning in your math test, you see a classmate copy an answer from another's paper.

_____ 10. Your sister used your brush without asking you.

_____ 11. Your little brother is climbing up a dresser by opening the drawers and standing on them.

_____ 12. A classmate brought a can of spray paint to school and is writing on the bathroom walls.

For each of the tattling situations above, talk about or role play better ways to work them out.

5

Blackout!

Miss Cooper turned the van into a parking space at the Morgandale Plaza Mall. The Fairfield Friends piled out and helped Miss Cooper.

Cameron had met Miss Cooper a few months ago when she first moved into Fairfield Court. Since then, the rest of the friends had gotten to know her. Sometimes Miss Cooper took them for ice cream or to the library. Though paralyzed from the waist down from a diving accident, she could still drive. Her van was specially made with hand controls to drive and brake.

After Cameron and Ceely had helped Miss Cooper into her electric wheelchair, they hurried across the parking lot. It was bitterly cold out, and the wind was getting stronger.

"Thanks for bringing us all to the mall to

shop for Christmas gifts," said Min when they got inside.

"You're quite welcome, Min," answered Miss Cooper. "But I brought you with me mostly so you guys can carry all the stuff I buy." She winked at them, then laughed loudly. The six friends laughed along with her.

"Hey!" exclaimed Ceely. "The mall sure is decorated."

"Look at all the Christmas trees," added Roberto.

"Huh?" asked Cameron. They had just walked under a loudspeaker blaring "Jingle Bells" through the mall.

Roberto repeated what he'd said, and Cameron nodded. "The lights and tinsel sure are bright."

They followed Miss Cooper slowly up the mall, carefully moving through the crowds of people. At one end of the mall a choir was singing, and dozens of shoppers had stopped to listen. As the group passed by, the singers began "Jolly Old St. Nicholas." It was a fitting song because just past them sat Santa Claus on a red velvet throne. The line of kids waiting to tell him what they wanted for Christmas stretched down the mall.

"Let's go to the Hosanna Christian Bookstore," said Miss Cooper.

"At least in there it will feel like the real meaning of Christmas," Ceely said.

"Yeah," agreed Valerie.

"You are so right," said Miss Cooper. "In fact, if you look around at all this holiday hoopla, not one decoration or display has anything to do with the birth of Christ."

Just as she finished her words, they arrived in front of the Christian bookstore. Miss Cooper sighed. "Boy, is this discouraging," she said.

"What do you mean?" asked Hutch.

"Oh, just that the Christian bookstore has these big displays of shirts, mugs, and other gifts to pull in customers. The Bible display is stuck in the far corner of the store."

Inside the store, Miss Cooper bought a new Bible for her brother and some Christian adventure books for her niece and nephew. Hutch and Valerie each bought a present for their mothers.

With their purchases made, they again joined the confusion and crowds in the main mall. They noticed a lot of the noise came from the toy store. Dozens of kids ran through the store grabbing toys off the shelves to show their parents what they wanted for Christmas.

Then, without any warning at all, the lights in the mall went out. Cries and screams filled the hall as everyone stopped where they were.

"Whoa," said Roberto. "I can't see anything."

"I'm scared," Valerie said.

"I feel like I've been stuck inside a piece of chocolate fudge," said Hutch.

"Why did the lights go out?" asked Ceely.

"Probably the wind outside," explained Cameron. "It was blowing pretty hard when we came in. It could have snapped a power line."

Some lights flickered on. "Ahh," said relieved people up and down the mall.

"Those are the backup lights," Miss Cooper explained. "They aren't too bright, but we can still—"

Shrieks and groans echoed again through the huge mall. The backup lights had gone out, too. The only light anywhere came from the red exit signs, not nearly enough to see by.

Worry and panic began to spread among the shoppers. Kids started to cry.

"Miss Cooper," said Min, fear in her voice, "what do we do now? There's no light at all."

Miss Cooper chuckled softly. "Min, honey, there's always light for us. Of course, it's not always a light we can see with our eyes." She stopped briefly. "Maybe the rest of the people here need to know that."

Miss Cooper cleared her voice loudly. "Attention, please," she called. "Attention."

The mall became completely still except for a few crying babies.

"I don't know what's wrong with the lights, but I'm sure someone is working on them. So let's not get upset. After all, we still have light with us. John 8:12 in the Bible says, 'Jesus is the light of the world.' "

"Right on, sister," came a voice up the mall.

"Light we can see is for our eyes and can

easily go out. But God gave us a light by sending Jesus, His Son. His light is light for the heart. So if you stay focused on His light, and not the light from Christmas trees, shiny tinsel, and bright store signs, you're never in complete darkness. After all, Christmas is named for Christ. He's the reason we celebrate Christmas."

When Miss Cooper finished, soft voices began telling others what she had said. Within a few minutes, everyone in the mall had heard Miss Cooper's message.

"Wow!" said Cameron softly. "That was so great of you to say what you did."

The rest of the Fairfield Friends agreed.

"Look!" yelled someone from somewhere down the mall.

"Yeah, right," came a response. "Look at what?"

"Look up at the skylight in the middle of the mall."

Once again, the stilled people passed word from one to the other to look up at the large glass opening in the roof of the mall.

"I see it!" Hutch exclaimed. "The moonlight is shining through it."

"Ooh," said Valerie.

Sure enough, the clouds had parted outside,

and a beam of moonlight streamed into the mall.

"Did you see what the moonlight landed on?" Roberto asked.

"It's shining right into the Hosanna Christian Bookstore," answered Min excitedly.

"But even more than that," added Cameron. "When the light shines through the glass window, it sort of bends and shifts. It's shining directly on . . ."

"The display of Bibles," finished Ceely.

"Awesome," Hutch said.

Miss Cooper chuckled softly.

For several seconds, there was complete stillness and peace. Suddenly, there came a flash, and then another, as the bright lights of the mall flickered on. And like a huge machine that had been turned back on, the mall came to life again. Miss Cooper and the friends watched the renewed activity around them.

"I guess everything's back to the way it was," said Ceely.

"I'm not so sure about that," said Miss Cooper. She pointed across the mall. "Look."

The bookstore had moved its Bible display out of the store and in front of the shirts and mugs. People were clustered around, looking at the Bibles. A line had formed at the cash register.

When the group passed the toy store, parents scolded their children for wanting too much. At the end of the mall, the group of singers was joyfully singing "Sweet Little Jesus Boy," an old song from Civil War days.

As the Fairfield Friends and Miss Cooper reached the door to the parking lot, they turned around and looked back up the mall.

"I think a miracle just happened here tonight," said Cameron.

"No, Cameron," said Miss Cooper. "The miracle happened a long, long time ago in a stable in Bethlehem."

As they walked through the door, the melody of "Silent Night" playing over the mall's loudspeakers drifted out the door with them. And overhead, the stars shined brilliantly.

Things to Think About

Describe the mall before its lights went out.

_____

_____

What light did Miss Cooper tell the mall shoppers about?

_____

_____

What was the mall like after the lights came back on?

_____

_____

Read John 8:12. What does the light of Jesus do for people?

_____

_____

_____

Read 1 John 1:5–7. Why should Christians live in "the Light"?

_____

_____

_____

Read Luke 2:1–12. What was the miracle that happened in the stable in Bethlehem?

_____

_____

Let's Act It Out!

Memorize John 8:12.

During the Christmas season, make your favorite cake and sing "Happy Birthday" to Jesus.

Make a "God's Light Never Fails" paper. Fold a piece of white construction paper into thirds the long way, then open it up and fold it into thirds the short way. When you open it up, the paper should be divided into nine equal rectangles. In each of the eight outside sections, draw an example of a different kind of light such as a lamp, a candle, or a lantern. In the middle square, draw a picture to represent the light of Jesus. You could draw a sun or maybe a heart with a little flame in it. Now take a piece of black paper and fold it into nine sections like the white paper. Cut out the middle square. Lay the black paper on top of the white paper and fasten the top edge with tape or staples. What happens to all the light sources you drew? Which light still shines?

6

A Real Rat

H ere's your ruler, Kevin," said Hutch.

Kevin took the ruler, took a deep breath, and then ran outside. Ten seconds later, he ran back. "It's this far now!" Kevin said excitedly as he pointed to the number four on the ruler.

It was the day after Christmas, and it had been snowing since early morning. Hutch, Ceely, and their cousins, Kevin and Bridget, who'd spent Christmas with them, sat in the family room playing with some things they'd gotten for Christmas. Every few minutes, one of them got up and looked out the window at the falling snow. But looking wasn't good enough for four-year-old Kevin. He ran outside every half hour with a ruler to measure how much had fallen.

That afternoon, Kevin's ruler completely

disappeared in the snow. When Snowball ran into the yard, she disappeared, too. Only the tip of her black tail stuck up from the snow. Everyone in the Coleman house was excited except Mr. Coleman. He kept looking at the driveway and shaking his head.

Hutch, Kevin, and Bridget got out their snow pants, coats, hats, and mittens and began dressing to go out to play. As Hutch pulled on his boots, the phone rang. Ceely, who was in the kitchen baking cookies, answered it.

"It's for you, Hutch," she yelled. "It's your friend Todd."

Hutch ran to the kitchen and picked up the phone. "Oh hi, Todd," said Hutch. "Yeah, the snow's great. . . . Sledding? Tomorrow? Yeah, sure. Sounds like fun. . . . Wow, s'mores will be awesome. . . . OK. See you then."

Hutch hung up the phone and turned to leave when the phone rang again. It was Jeff, another friend from school. "Great snow, huh?. . . . Skiing? Tomorrow?. . . . And we'll spend the night at the ski lodge? Hold on. I'll ask."

Hutch put the phone down and went to search for his mother. *Skiing sounds like a lot more fun than sledding*, he thought.

He was back in a minute. "It's OK. I can go,"

Hutch said to Jeff excitedly. "All right. See you at 8:00." Hutch hung up the phone.

"Aren't you forgetting something?" Ceely asked as she slid oatmeal cookies onto a cooling rack. "Or are you able to ski and sled in two different places at the same time?"

"Oh, Todd won't mind," said Hutch. "I can go sledding with him any old time."

"But he called first," Ceely said. "You better call back and cancel with Jeff."

"I will later," said Hutch. "Right now I'm so hot with all this stuff on I'll probably melt all the snow." He hurried out the kitchen door into a yard full of snow and joined Kevin and Bridget.

All afternoon, while Hutch played in the snow, he thought about the fun he'd have on the ski slopes the next day. But then he remembered what Ceely said. That evening, Hutch continued to fight with himself over whether to go sledding or skiing.

Finally, just before bedtime, Hutch cancelled his sledding plans with his friend. "I'm sorry," he said into the phone, "but I can't go sledding tomorrow. Maybe another time, OK? See ya, Todd."

Hutch hung up the phone. He raced up the steps two at a time to his room and began packing for his ski trip.

While Hutch packed, Kevin, who was sharing Hutch's room while visiting, walked in and flopped onto Hutch's bed. He picked up Hutch's *God's Amazing World* magazine and flipped through the pages.

"Hutch, would you read me this story?" asked Kevin. "It's about Noah's ark. It's really short."

"Yeah, OK," Hutch said as he snapped his suitcase shut. He picked up the magazine and began to read.

After Hutch finished, Kevin turned to him. "How do we know for sure that God won't bring another flood to kill everything?"

"Because He says He won't," answered Hutch. "Besides, He made rainbows to remind us of His promise."

"But He could change His mind," said Kevin.

"No way," Hutch said. "God always does what He says. He's faithful to us."

"What does faithful mean?" Kevin asked.

"It means . . . well . . . um . . ." stammered Hutch. *How on earth do you explain faithfulness to a four-year-old?* he wondered. He looked at the end of the story in the parents' help box. It listed several Bible verses.

Hutch grabbed his Bible off his nightstand and looked up the first one. "First Corinthians 4:2," said Hutch. " 'Now it is required that those who have been given a trust must prove faithful' " (NIV).

"Huh?" asked Kevin.

Hutch sighed. "That means that if you tell a person you'll do something, that person trusts you to be faithful and do it. If you don't do what you promised, you're a real rat." All at once, the words Hutch spoke began to tumble around in his brain.

"Now go to sleep," said Hutch a little angrily. Kevin crawled into his sleeping bag and Hutch got into his bed. He yanked the covers over himself, but he couldn't sleep. He rolled and flopped around all night.

———

The next morning, Hutch's excitement for the ski trip was gone. He packed and repacked his things in his suitcase. He couldn't get his stuff to fit right.

Ceely passed by his room and saw Hutch's suitcase on his bed. She shook her head at him. "Boy, aren't you a rat," she said.

Hutch sat on his bed. His stomach didn't feel too great. He finally went down to breakfast, but he couldn't eat anything. He looked at the clock. The minute hand kept inching its way around the dial. The hour hand was closing in fast on the eight.

Hutch zipped up his ski jacket and stood at the front window. Soon, a car pulled up at the curb and honked. Hutch picked up his suitcase. Then he put it down again and ran out the door to the car.

A minute later, the car pulled away. Hutch waved and then walked back into the house.

Ceely gave him a half smile before going up-stairs.

"What's wrong, Hutch?" Mom asked as she walked into the living room. "Why aren't you going skiing with Jeff? Don't you feel well?"

"Oh, I feel great," said Hutch. "It's just that I told Todd I'd come over and sled with him to-day."

"You just remembered?" asked Mom suspiciously.

"No, I just thought about faithfulness . . . and rats," Hutch answered. He picked up his suitcase and took it back to his room. Then he hurried to the phone to call Todd.

Todd and Hutch spent all morning sledding down a big hill near Todd's house. They tried out his new toboggan. It flew like a jet down the hill. They raced each other with sleds and saucers, too.

Later on, when they were finally exhausted, they headed inside. After toasting marshmal-lows over the fire in the fireplace, they placed them between chocolate bar halves and gra-ham crackers. Then they squished it all to-gether.

"Wow, these s'mores are great," said Todd.

"They sure are," Hutch agreed. He finished his and licked the melted chocolate and gooey

marshmallows off his fingers. Then they each
made another s'more.

Things to Think About

How did Hutch feel when he got up in the morning to go skiing? Why?

_____

_____

What did the story of Noah teach Hutch about faithfulness?

_____

_____

How did Hutch show his faithfulness to Todd?

_____

_____

Read Psalm 117:2 and 145:13b. Describe the faithfulness of God.

_____

_____

_____

Read Proverbs 18:24 and 20:6. What is a faithful friend?

_____

_____

_____

Read Ruth 1:3–9, 14–17. How was Ruth a
faithful daughter-in-law to Naomi?

_____

_____

Let's Act It Out!

Memorize 1 Corinthians 4:2.

List ways you can be a faithful son/daughter,
brother/sister, friend, Christian.

_____

_____

Make a doorknob rainbow. Using markers,
crayons, or paints, make a rainbow on a piece
of paper. Start with purple on the bottom followed by blue, green, yellow, orange, and red.
Cut it out, make a hole in the top, and tie a
piece of yarn or string through it. Now hang
it on your door to remind you of God's faithfulness and your faithfulness to others.

The Race

Roberto, Min, and Valerie walked from Fairfield Elementary to Morgandale High School. They were talking about the upcoming Field Day, the biggest event of the school year.

"I am so glad it finally stopped raining," said Roberto, "so I can practice my sprints for Field Day."

"And I'm glad we got out of school early today," said Min. "It gives me some extra time to practice for Field Day before ballet class tonight." She turned to Valerie, who was busy jumping over puddles as they walked down the street. "I'm guessing that you're going to enter the long jump?"

"You're right," answered Valerie, leaping over another puddle.

When the three friends arrived at the high

school stadium and track, Valerie headed to the inside area to practice long jumps. Min and Roberto continued onto the track.

"Why don't we race down to where the track begins to turn?" suggested Roberto.

The two of them lined up side by side.

"On your mark," started Roberto. "Get set. GO!"

They both charged down the track. After several yards, Roberto began to pull ahead of Min. All at once, Roberto fell.

"Owwww!" he yelled.

Min hurried over to him. "Are you all right?" she asked.

"Aww, I pulled a muscle in my leg," Roberto answered. He cradled his thigh in his hands.

Valerie soon joined them, and Min told her what had happened.

"Why do things always go wrong?" Roberto asked angrily. "I might as well give up and not even run in the race."

———

Two days later, though still limping a little, Roberto and Grandpop attended Wednesday night prayer meeting as usual. Before the Bible study started, Pastor Conrad told the members that the Altland family's house had been

flooded because of all the recent rain. The small creek they lived beside had overflowed its banks, and they'd had a foot of water in the first floor.

"The Altlands really need our prayer support now," said Pastor Conrad, "but I also think they could use some help with the cleanup. If any of you can spare some time over the next few days, I'm sure they'd appreciate it."

On the way home from church, Roberto asked Grandpop if he could help with the cleanup at the Altlands'. Grandpop thought it was a wonderful idea as long as Roberto was careful with his leg. Roberto said that he would be.

———

The next day, when Grandpop pulled up at Fairfield Elementary, Min and Valerie were there as well.

"I told Min and Valerie about the Altlands," explained Roberto. "They'd like to help, too."

"Sounds good," Grandpop replied. "I'll call Mrs. Stevens and Grandmother Hing when we get to the Altlands to let them know they're with us."

When they all arrived at the Altland house, they couldn't believe the first floor. Although the water had gone down, it had left a coating of mud over everything to a height of one foot.

"Hello, Mr. and Mrs. Altland," said Grandpop when they found them cleaning the kitchen. He introduced Min and Valerie.

"Where would you like us to help?" Min asked.

"Sally and Keith are in the family room. They might need some help in there. And my brother Tom is in the dining room."

Grandpop used the phone and then joined

Tom Altland in the dining room. Roberto, Min, and Valerie went to the family room to help Sally and Keith, the Altlands' teenaged children.

"Hi, Sally, Keith," said Roberto. "These are my school friends Min and Valerie."

After greetings were exchanged, Keith gave them each a towel and showed them what they could start to clean.

"Boy, this is really awful," said Roberto as he wiped mud from an end table. "You guys must be really upset over having a flood in your house."

Sally shrugged. "Things like this are bound to happen sometimes," she said.

"That's why it's good to be prepared, because you never know what might come your way in life," added Keith.

Roberto, Min, and Valerie looked at one another and frowned slightly, not understanding what they meant.

"Fantastic!" shouted Sally suddenly. "My devotion notebook and Bible didn't get wet." She lifted them off the second shelf of the bookcase, a couple inches above the flood line.

"My photo album from King's Kids Christian Camp last summer wasn't so lucky," said Keith. He held up an album, bent and muddy.

"I guess I'll have to get new pictures made and make another album."

"How's it going in here?" asked Mr. Altland as he walked in.

"Great, Dad," answered Keith.

"What a mess," said Mr. Altland, shaking his head and chuckling slightly. "But it's not enough to stop us from running our race, is it?"

"No way, Dad," answered Sally.

"Race?" asked Roberto. "What race?"

Mr. Altland smiled. "Oh, I'm just referring to First Corinthians 9:24 and 25, Roberto, which says that we must 'run the race that is before us and never give up.' The writer compares living the Christian life to running a race."

"And we're able to run the Christian 'race' by training and preparing for it just like an athlete does for a sporting event," added Sally. "We go to Sunday school and church, have devotions, read our Bibles, pray, and attend Christian camps and youth group."

"By training for the Christian life this way," continued Mr. Altland, "you add to your spiritual knowledge and strength. You learn that God is always with you, and that He's working things out for your good. You also know He'll comfort you and encourage you. So when tough times come along, you're able to continue your Christian race. At the end, you get a prize, which for the Christian is eternal life."

———

On the way to school the next day, Roberto, Min, and Valerie made plans to practice again for Field Day after school.

"My leg is OK now," said Roberto. "But I'm going to warm up and stretch my muscles first. Then I'm going to jog short distances and work up to the sprints. I know I need to train for my race the right way. Then I'll be ready to run the best race I can."

"That sounds like good planning," said Min.

"I agree," Valerie said. "I'll bet the Altlands would be pleased with our Field Day preparations, too."

———

When Field Day finally arrived three weeks later, Min won second place in a long race. Valerie won third in the long jump. And Roberto won the 100-yard dash.

As they walked home, they talked excitedly about the day's events, their ribbons fluttering in the breeze. When they reached Hillside

Drive, Roberto said he needed to swing over to the grocery store to get a loaf of bread for Grandpop. Min and Valerie went along.

They turned down Spring Garden Street and then cut across the parking lot to the Shopping Giant store. All at once, Roberto saw movement out of the corner of his eye. He jerked his head in that direction and saw a grocery cart full of bags rolling away from a lady loading her car. The cart began to gather speed as it rolled down the sloping parking lot. It was headed right for a small child!

Roberto blasted across the lot at full speed. Just before the cart rolled into the child, Roberto caught the handle on the shopping cart and yanked it to a stop. Several people in the lot clapped. Both the toddler's mother and the owner of the runaway cart thanked Roberto.

"That was some sprint," said Min when she and Valerie caught up to Roberto.

"It pays to be prepared," he said, smiling.

The girls patted Roberto on the back. Then they entered the grocery store and began a search for the bread.

Things to Think About

What happened to Roberto the first day at the track? Why?

_____

_____

Why did the Altland family have the strength and courage to deal with the flood?

_____

_____

How did proper training help the Fairfield Friends during and after Field Day?

_____

_____

Read 2 Timothy 4:7–8. Why is living the Christian life like running a race?

_____

_____

Read 1 Peter 1:3–7 and James 1:12. Why should we never give up when tough times come along?

_____

_____

_____

Read 1 Corinthians 9:24–25. Why is winning the Christian "crown" more important than winning an earthly crown?

_____

_____

Let's Act It Out!

Memorize 2 Timothy 4:7.

Play the "Win the Crown Game." Take a piece of paper and divide it lengthwise with a ruler and pencil, forming one column for each player. Now divide the paper into ten vertical rows. Draw a crown in the last block of each column. Using paper clips, buttons, or other markers, each player starts at the end of a column. After numbering pieces of paper from 1–20, each player moves ahead, back, or not at all according to the numbered situation he draws. The first person to end on the crown with an exact number of moves wins.

1. You memorized a Bible verse. Move ahead two spaces.
2. You drew pictures during church. Move back one space.

3. You encouraged others on your soccer team. Move ahead one space.

4. You didn't warm up before your gymnastics class. Don't move at all.

5. You got a little tired in the middle of a race in gym class so you stopped. Go back to start.

6. You pushed someone out of the way while hurrying into your class before the bell rang. Move back two spaces.

7. You cheated on a test to get a better grade on your report card. Move back three spaces.

8. You did your devotions. Move ahead three spaces.

9. You tried to start a race before the starter said go. Don't move at all.

10. You spent a week at a Christian camp. Move ahead three spaces.

11. You said you felt sick so you could skip youth group. Move back one space.

12. You forgot to pray. Don't move at all.

13. You asked a question you had in Sunday school. Move ahead three spaces.

14. You tried your hardest in a game in gym class. Move ahead one space.

15. You finished your homework so you could attend prayer meeting. Move

ahead two spaces.

16. You quit ballet because you didn't like it when the teacher corrected you. Move back two spaces.
17. You went to bed without arguing with your parents. Move ahead one space.
18. You didn't do well on a test, so you cut back on your TV time and increased your study time. Move ahead two spaces.
19. Your friends tried to get you to do something wrong but you refused, even though they made fun of you. Move ahead three spaces.
20. Your house was destroyed in an earthquake, but you kept your faith in God and had the strength and courage to deal with your loss. Move ahead four spaces.

8

Zapped!

I can't believe it! thought Cameron. *How could I not have had the highest grades in my class for the year? How did Trevor Jameson beat me?*

It was the last day of school, and Cameron had just left Foster Academy's honor assembly. When the award for the year's highest grades was announced, Cameron was halfway out of his seat before he realized he hadn't won.

As Cameron climbed onto his school bus for the ride home, he was still thinking about his loss. *It must have been that B I got on my book report in English,* he thought as he flopped into a seat. *But Trevor's wasn't all that great.*

When Cameron arrived home, he slammed the front door. Then he growled at Justine to get out of his way before he stomped up the stairs to his room.

Cameron spent the rest of his day in his room. As the jealous feelings grew, he became angrier and more frustrated. He had a headache, and his stomach didn't feel too great.

Finally, Cameron got thirsty enough to go downstairs for a drink. As he entered the kitchen, he stopped quickly and stared at the floor. At first, it looked as if the floor itself was moving. Then Cameron realized something was moving on the floor. Ants!

Cameron called his mom to the kitchen, and she immediately called the Morgandale Pest Control Center. The exterminator, the person who destroys bugs, said he'd be over in an hour.

At 5:15, Cameron's dad drove in the driveway from work. Pulling in behind him was a van with lettering on the side. It said "Terry the Terminator. If I don't zap all your bugs, I'll be back!"

Terry walked silently into the Parker kitchen and looked at the ants for a minute. He frowned, nodded his head, and strolled back to his van. He returned a few minutes later carrying a large metal can with a spray nozzle on the top.

"You have an ant problem," he said to the

Parker family. "But my bug blaster will zap them."

For the next half hour, Terry the Terminator sprayed the baseboards, the closets, the cupboards, and the pantry. Then he moved upstairs to spray those closets and any other places ants might sneak in. Since they didn't want to get in Terry's way while he sprayed, the Parker family gathered in the family room.

"Those ants give me the creeps," said Justine. She shivered slightly.

"How on earth did they get in here?" asked Mom. "And why were there so many of them?"

"Oh, they can slide in anywhere, anytime," Dad answered. "Once a few get in, more follow. Unless you zap them, as Terry puts it, the number keeps growing until they take over the house." He paused for a minute while he thought. "You know," he continued, "these ants remind me about sin."

"How, Dad?" asked Philip.

"Well, sin slips into our lives just like ants get into a house. If we don't get rid of the sin by confessing it, it can take over and destroy us." He picked up his Bible on the couch and flipped open to James. "Here it is," he said. "Chapter 1, verse 15. 'The sin grows and brings death,' meaning the death of our souls."

A figure at the doorway interrupted Dad. "I zapped the ants," said Terry. "And sucked up their bodies with my vacuum."

Mr. Parker paid Terry and thanked him. While the rest of the family scattered to other parts of the house, Cameron remained frozen in a chair in the family room. He felt his Dad's words crawling through him like . . . well, like ants.

Dear God, began Cameron. *I know I sinned when I let my jealousy and anger grow because I didn't win the award at school. Forgive me, and help me not to sin. Amen.*

Cameron felt clean and fresh all at once. His headache was gone, and he suddenly realized he was starving. "Mom!" yelled Cameron. "What's for supper?"

————

A few days later, while Cameron was playing in his bedroom, he heard a *BUZZZ*. He looked toward the sound and saw a bee flying around the room. *How did he get in here?* Cameron wondered. He shrugged. *Who cares? What's one little bee? Besides, Terry's ant spray will probably kill it and any other bees that show up.*

The next evening, Cameron saw another

bee, but again he didn't pay much attention to it. He was just excited to meet the rest of the Fairfield Friends for a bike ride.

An hour later, Cameron hurried into the driveway on his bike. He was twenty minutes late. He found his parents waiting for him in the family room. "Sorry I'm late," rushed Cameron before they could say anything. "My chain fell off my bike, and it took a while to get back on."

Since his chain had fallen off twice before, his parents believed him and didn't punish him for being late.

Whew! thought Cameron. *Am I ever lucky my chain has fallen off before. Even though it didn't this time, it was the perfect cover-up for being late.*

As Cameron got ready for bed, though, he didn't feel quite right. He felt like ants were crawling on him again.

In the middle of the night, Cameron's eyes popped open. Loud buzzing filled the room. "Aaahhh!" hollered Cameron. "BEES! HELP!"

Cameron swatted every which way through the air with his arms. It felt like an army of bees had taken over his room.

The light flicked on suddenly. "Cameron, c'mon," said his dad urgently.

Cameron ran through the open door, and his dad slammed it behind him. Then he stuffed a towel in the crack at the bottom.

"Are you OK, Cameron?" Mom asked, stumbling sleepily down the hall. "Were you stung?"

"No," replied Cameron. "I don't think so."

"You'll have to sleep the rest of the night in the guest room," said Dad. "I'll call the exterminator in the morning."

————

At 9:00 the next morning, the doorbell rang. Cameron opened the door.

"I'm back," said Terry the Terminator.

Cameron took Terry to his bedroom. After putting on his bee suit for protection, Terry entered the room. A minute later, he was back.

"You have a bee problem," he said. "A big bee problem. There's a hive behind the wall in your closet, in the attic space. You should have called me when you saw the first bee. I could have zapped them."

"But you sprayed for the ants," said Cameron. "Why didn't that kill the bees, too?"

"Bees are different from ants. One kind of spray doesn't work on both. You have to get rid of each pest with a separate spray."

Cameron nodded, now realizing why he felt like he had bees and ants crawling on him. His lie to his parents about being late hadn't been forgiven simply because he'd confessed his earlier sins of anger and jealousy.

Cameron knew what he had to do. First, he asked God to forgive him for lying. Then he confessed to his parents and asked them for their forgiveness.

That evening, after Cameron had gotten into bed, he realized he hadn't said his prayers. But being tired, he decided to skip them and say them in the morning.

All at once, Cameron heard a soft buzzing.

He jumped out of bed and turned on his light. A monster mosquito buzzed around his head. Cameron stood back, lined up the mosquito between his hands, and then slapped them together.

SMACK!

After wiping his hands on his shirt, Cameron crawled back into bed. But before he lay down to sleep, he said his prayers. Then he drifted off to sleep in a still and silent room.

Cave Hill Treasure

Things to Think About

What were Cameron's sins?

_____

_____

Why didn't Cameron say anything about the
bees in his room? What happened?

_____

_____

_____

How did Cameron learn about sin and getting
rid of it?

_____

_____

Read Proverbs 28:13; Psalm 51:3; and Romans
6:22–23. Why must you confess your sin?

_____

_____

_____

Read 1 John 1:9; James 5:16; and Daniel 9:3–
4. Who must you confess your sins to?

_____

_____

_____

Read James 4:8 and Titus 2:11–12. How can you reduce the number of sins in your life?

_____

_____

Let's Act It Out!

Memorize Daniel 9:4.

Make a "Bugs on a Log" snack. Clean a rib of celery and spread peanut butter in the groove. Put raisins on the peanut butter and pretend they're bugs. Now take a big bite. Act out how you'd feel if you ate this and they were real bugs. That's exactly how you should feel when you sin.

Make your very own bug. Cut out three cups of an egg carton. Paint or decorate the "body" with markers. Push pipe cleaners into two sections for the legs and two in the head for antennae. Keep your bug on your dresser to remind you to "zap" those sins.

9

Flies and Tomatoes

Valerie dove in the water and swam down the pool. When she crawled out at the other end, her coach stopped her.

"Valerie, you're looking a little lazy out there today," said Coach Lipman. "You need to work harder during practice so you'll be ready for our meet tomorrow."

I don't need to work that hard, thought Valerie. *My freestyle time is great, and my breast stroke has really improved. Besides, we haven't lost a swim meet to Cumberland Township Pool for years.* But since the coach was watching her when she dove back in, Valerie swam a little faster.

When practice was over, Valerie hopped on her bike for the ride home. As she pedaled down the road, she was quickly reminded of the leak in her back tire. With every bump, Valerie's tire flattened down to the metal rim.

"Valerie!" exclaimed Mom when she saw her ride in the driveway. "Why haven't you gotten that leak fixed yet? I've told you several times that Mr. Henry down the street will gladly patch it for you."

"Sorry, Mom," Valerie answered, shrugging. "I just haven't gotten around to it."

Mom sighed and continued. "Now, you know the progressive dinner is tonight."

"Yeah," answered Valerie, "but I forget what it is exactly."

"A progressive dinner," Mom explained, "is when a group of people eat the different parts of a meal at different people's houses. The adult Sunday school class is having soup at Mrs. Kepner's, two doors down. Then the group will come here for salad before continuing on to other houses for the main course and dessert."

"That sounds like so much fun," said Valerie.

"It is fun," agreed her mom. "But it also takes a lot of work to prepare all the food. That's why Mrs. Kepner and I are helping each other make the soup and salad at her house this afternoon. While I'm there, I need you to take out the trash on the patio and bring in some tomatoes."

Valerie had planted a few tomato plants this year in the far corner of the backyard after agreeing to water and weed them. She had even offered to provide the tomatoes for tonight's dinner.

"I trust that your tomatoes are ripe and juicy," Mom said, smiling. "I haven't stopped down at your garden in a while."

I haven't checked them for a while, either, thought Valerie.

That afternoon, Valerie flopped down in front of the TV after her mom and Bonnie had left. Her mom had said that she'd be home around 5:30, just before the guests arrived. Since she had plenty of time to get things done, Valerie found a good show and settled back.

After two more shows, Valerie looked at her watch. It said 5:15!

"Oh no!" yelled Valerie. She raced through the house and down the backyard to her tomato plants. But when she got to them, her eyes opened in horror. There were weeds everywhere. The plants were dried out, and the tomatoes were tiny.

Valerie grabbed the few good tomatoes she could find and ran back to the kitchen. She

washed them and laid them on the counter. At that moment, her mom and Bonnie walked in. Her mom carried a big bowl of salad in front of her.

"Hi, Valerie," said Mom. "The group is at the Kepners' eating their soup. They'll be here in a few minutes." She put down the bowl of salad on the kitchen table. "Let's get those toma—" Valerie's mom stopped in the middle of the word. "Valerie," said Mom. "Are those all the tomatoes you were able to get?"

Valerie nodded.

"But now I don't have enough for the salad."

Valerie hung her head. "Sorry," she mumbled.

The doorbell rang.

"The group is here," said her mom. "Let's take them to the patio."

Yikes! thought Valerie. *The trash!*

When the guests arrived on the patio, every nose wrinkled as the smell from the garbage can hit them. It was awful. Even worse were the fat black flies that buzzed around it and sat on the tables and chairs.

"Sorry, folks. The trash was supposed to be taken out." She glanced at Valerie. "Why don't we move inside to the living room for our salads?"

When the guests had gone, Valerie's mom had a long talk with her about her laziness. "Proverbs 19:15 says, 'Lazy people sleep a lot. Idle people will go hungry.' Everything that happened today resulted from your laziness. First, there weren't enough tomatoes to eat because you haven't taken care of them. And then I sent our guests onto a stinky, fly-covered patio. That was really embarrassing, Valerie. There will be no TV for a week, and you'll have extra chores to do. Now get to bed. You need your rest for your swim meet tomorrow."

As Valerie got ready for bed, she giggled a little. *I wasn't embarrassed about the flies,* she thought. *I thought it was sort of funny.*

———

The next morning, Valerie groggily opened her eyes to slits as her mom shook her. "Valerie," she said. "It's time to get up."

"Umm-hmm," Valerie mumbled as she sat up in bed.

"Remember," she continued. "I have to take Bonnie for her checkup at the doctor. You'll have to hurry if you want me to drop you off at the pool."

After her Mom left the room, Valerie fell back onto her bed. *I hate getting up early,* she thought. *Just a few more minutes won't hurt.* Valerie drifted back to sleep.

"Valerie!"

Valerie bolted upright in bed.

"I told you to get up twenty minutes ago," Mom said. "I'm ready to go now. I can't be late for Bonnie's appointment."

Valerie scrambled out of bed and quickly pulled on her swimsuit. "It's OK, Mom. I'll just ride my bike. I can make it in time."

But the minute Valerie saw her bike, she remembered she'd never gotten the leak fixed yesterday. After a couple blocks, Valerie's tire was totally flat. And when the tire came off the rim, Valerie was forced to get off.

Valerie wheeled her bike by the handlebars as fast as she could go. *I know I'm going to be late for the meet. I just hope I don't miss my races.*

As Valerie approached the pool entrance, she suddenly heard her name announced over the loudspeaker. Valerie raced in and up to the starting blocks. When the starting gun fired, Valerie dove in and came up swimming freestyle. She stroked down the pool to the finish.

When she popped up out of the water, she heard loud laughter. Valerie looked behind her at the other swimmers who were swimming . . . breaststroke.

I am so embarrassed, thought Valerie as she climbed out of the pool.

In a few minutes, the man on the loudspeaker announced the winners. He also said that Valerie Stevens had been disqualified for swimming the wrong stroke. Again, Valerie heard laughter.

I don't think it's that funny, she thought. *At least I have another race. I think I can win that one.*

But near the end of her next race, Valerie tired out and came in third. When the final results had been totaled, Morgandale Community Pool had lost the meet by only five points.

As Valerie wheeled her bike home, tears stung her eyes. *If I hadn't been so lazy, maybe the team could have won.*

After parking her bike, Valerie weeded her garden and watered her tomatoes. Then she took her bike to Mr. Henry to fix her tire. And that afternoon, Valerie returned to the pool and practiced her swimming.

Cave Hill Treasure

Things to Think About

In what ways was Valerie lazy?

_____

_____

How did her laziness affect others?

_____

_____

How did her laziness affect her?

_____

_____

Read Ecclesiastes 10:18; 2 Thessalonians 3:10;
Proverbs 19:15; and 24:30–34. What happens
to the lazy person?

_____

_____

_____

Read Proverbs 10:4 and 1 Thessalonians 4:11–
12. What are the results of hard work?

_____

_____

_____

Read Colossians 3:23. How can you overcome laziness?

_____

_____

Let's Act It Out!

Memorize Proverbs 19:15.

Draw a picture of yourself doing some kind of "work."

Each week, write down the list of jobs or chores you have to do around the house. Surprise your parents by doing all of them without being reminded.

If the area where you live allows for gardening, plant some flowers or vegetables with an adult's help. Or buy a plant from a greenhouse to keep indoors. Make sure you are responsible for the care of the plants. What happens when you take care of them each day? What will happen if you don't?

10

Cave Hill Treasure

The wrecking crane slammed into the old house again. Bricks and wood flew everywhere as the house broke apart. Along the edge of the property, a rope had been placed to keep people from getting too close. Behind one area of rope stood the Fairfield Friends.

"It's so great that people are allowed to watch them tear down this creepy old house," Hutch added.

"I think it's a little sad," said Min.

"Me too," Ceely said. "After all, Cletus Smith built this house himself."

"Yeah, but he was so strange," said Roberto. "Grandpop said he never left the house. He even had his groceries delivered to him."

"Well, he's been dead for years," said Cameron. "And now some company bought the land to build a bunch of office buildings here."

The crane smashed into the house again. A cloud of dust rose. It swirled and drifted toward the Fairfield Friends. When the dust settled, a folded piece of paper landed right at their feet.

"What's this?" asked Min, stooping down to pick up the paper.

"It must have blown out of the wall on that last blast," Hutch replied.

Min opened the paper while the friends gathered around.

"It's a map!" exclaimed Cameron excitedly. "It shows the cave at Cave Hill, just over by Pawnee Creek."

"Look!" said Ceely. "It shows different tunnels in the cave."

"And there's an X right here," Valerie said, pointing at the paper.

"Isn't there some story about a bank robber who hid money in the cave or something?" asked Ceely.

"I'm not sure," said Roberto. "But Grandpop might know."

The Fairfield Friends jumped on their bikes and hurried to Roberto's house. They found Ramone and Grandpop and showed them the map. Grandpop said there was an old, local story about Lewis the Robber who'd robbed a

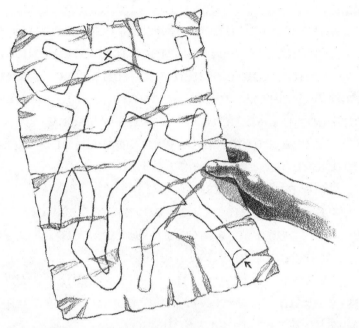

bank in the 1890s. Neither he nor the money was ever found. According to stories that had passed from person to person, he'd hidden the money in the cave at Cave Hill.

"Well, let's go look for it then," said Roberto.

Grandpop laughed. "I doubt there's really any treasure in the cave," he said.

"But it might be fun to go exploring in the cave a little," Ramone said. "It's perfectly safe," he assured Grandpop. "Ross and I have been inside the front room a couple times. In fact,

I'll give Ross a call and see if he wants to join us."

After the Fairfield Friends got permission from their parents, they met at the remains of the Smith house. Then they followed a path that led across the field, through some trees, and down a slope to the cave's opening.

"We're supposed to wait outside until Ross and Ramone get here," said Roberto.

Ten minutes passed.

"I don't want to wait anymore," said Cameron. "I want to search for the treasure."

"Me too," said Valerie.

"Can't we just go inside the front room?" asked Hutch.

"Well . . ." began Roberto.

"Oh, come on," said Cameron. "Ramone said it was safe."

They peeked inside the cave opening and then slipped inside. The air was cool and damp. And it was dark. Hutch, who'd brought a flashlight, turned it on and aimed it at Min, who had the map.

"The map shows passages leading from this room," said Min.

They followed the beam of Hutch's light with their eyes.

"There!" shouted Ceely. They saw a darkened tunnel leading out of the room.

"I'll bet the treasure is down that way," said Cameron.

"I hope we can find it," Min said.

"We could split it evenly," suggested Ceely.

"We'd all be rich," said Roberto. "Grand-pop could buy a new truck."

"And I could buy a new computer," Cameron said.

"Let's go," Valerie urged.

The Fairfield Friends started down the pitch black tunnel. Hutch's light made only a small path in the darkness. After walking a ways, the tunnel split into two more. The group turned to the left. The tunnel sloped down, then swung to the right. After following a couple more paths, the friends stopped.

"Does anyone know where we are?" asked Ceely.

"Check the map, Min," Cameron suggested.

"Did we go down this way or this way?" asked Roberto, pointing to two tunnels on the map.

"I'm not sure which way we went," said Min. "But I am sure I want to go back."

"I'm with you," Valerie said.

The rest agreed. They turned around and

started back, trying to remember exactly which way they'd come. Everything looked the same in the dark. They turned down one passage and stopped at a dead end. They tried another tunnel. But it was no use. They were completely lost inside the cave.

"Now what do we do?" asked Valerie.

"We'll have to wait for Ramone and Ross to find us," said Cameron.

They sat silently, huddled together in a group. An hour passed.

"What was that?" asked Roberto suddenly.

"What?" said Ceely.

"Shh," said Cameron.

"I hear voices," Min shouted.

The friends began yelling as loud as they could. Within a few minutes, a light bobbed from the end of a tunnel and shone on them. It was Ross and Ramone.

"Hurray!" hollered the friends.

The group followed a map Ross and Ramone had drawn on their way through the cave's passages to find the friends. Fifteen minutes later, they arrived back at the cave's entrance.

"I thought I told you to wait for us," scolded Ramone as they exited the cave into the brilliant sun.

The friends looked at one another.

"I guess we were blinded by thoughts of treasures and riches," said Roberto.

"We told you those were just stories," said Ramone.

"And besides," added Ross, "finding earthly treasure doesn't make a person rich. Matthew 6:19 says, 'Don't store treasures for yourselves here on earth.' A Christian should seek godly treasures such as wisdom, love, knowledge, and gentleness. These treasures will be stored in heaven for the Christian."

The following week, the friends got together again at the Smith property to see how much of the house was left. When they arrived, they saw nothing but two rows of the brick foundation sticking up from the ground. Hutch walked along the tops of them.

"Whoa!" he said suddenly, losing his balance. He looked down at the loose bricks and saw something sticking out. "Look at these," he said.

"Wow!" Ceely exclaimed. "It's a journal and a Bible."

"We know what's in the Bible," said Roberto. "Let's see what's in the journal."

They gathered around and began reading the entries in the small leather book. Each day's entry was as boring as the one before . . . until they got to the end.

"Unbelievable!" said Ceely, who was the fastest reader and finished the pages first. "Listen." She began to read.

June 12, 1948.

My sickness has gotten worse. I fear I am dying and have spent much time thinking about my life. I still remember that day I robbed the bank in town and escaped into the cave. I hid in one of the dark tunnels and buried the money there. After several days of wandering through the maze of passages, I found an opening into these very fields. I made a map of the tunnels so I could find my money again.

I grew a beard and changed my name to Cletus Smith. No one recognized me in town, so I decided to build a house here. I had more than enough money. But people began to wonder how I came into such wealth. I feared they would discover I was "Lewis the Robber" and put me in jail. I couldn't use my money. My treasure was useless.

For over fifty years I've stayed a prisoner here in my own house. I never go out and no one ever comes. Except one time, a man stopped and gave me a Bible. But I never read it. I couldn't see how some book would help me. And soon I'll die a poor man.

Ceely closed the journal and shook her head. "Lewis could have been rich if he'd bothered to read the Bible he'd been given."

"He'd have learned that knowing God and leading a Christian life is the only way to really be rich," added Min.

"And he could also have looked forward to a final treasure of eternal life in heaven," Hutch finished.

After talking a few more minutes, the Fairfield Friends nodded silently. Min pulled the map out of her pocket and put it inside the journal. Ceely and Roberto placed the journal back in the space between the rows of bricks. It would become part of the cement for a basement in a new office building. No one would ever be tempted to seek after the treasure in the cave.

Then the friends rode to Safe Harbor, the homeless shelter in Morgandale. Once inside, they put the Bible on a table in the lobby. The Fairfield Friends hoped that others could learn about true riches just as they had.

A Fairfield Friends Devotional Adventure

Things to Think About

What did the Fairfield Friends hope the treasure would give them?

_____

_____

What did the friends decide to do with the map, the journal, and the Bible? Why?

_____

_____

Why was Lewis the Robber "poor" and the Fairfield Friends "rich"?

_____

_____

Read Proverbs 10:2; Matthew 6:19; and Proverbs 23:5. What happens to earthly treasure?

_____

_____

Read 1 Timothy 6:17–19; Colossians 2:2; Psalm 119:14; Proverbs 2:1–5; and 22:4. What treasures should the Christian store up for heaven?

_____

_____

Cave Hill Treasure

Read Proverbs 27:19 (NIV). Explain how your heart shows where your treasure is.

_____

_____

Let's Act It Out!

Memorize Matthew 6:21.

Make a list of "earthly" treasures.

_____

_____

Unscramble the words below to discover the treasures Christians should seek after.

1. ssndnike
2. oyj
3. vloe
4. serceiv
5. ngcari
6. rshangi
7. wsimdo
8. nustndeangir
9. gorifveessn
10. pohe
11. hliimuty
12. cfonesisno
13. oonhr
14. oodgsesn
15. paeec

The answers are on page 127.

Make your own "treasure chest" out of an empty tissue box. Decorate the chest with paper, paint, markers, or glitter if you like. Tape or glue a piece of construction paper to the top edges of the box to form the curved chest lid. Now write each word you unscrambled above on a circle of yellow construction paper. Put your "treasure coins" into your "treasure chest." When you're tempted to seek after earthly treasures, open your treasure chest and check out your heavenly treasures. If you think of more heavenly treasures, add them to your treasure chest.

Answers

CHAPTER ONE

Paying back a wrong for a wrong simply makes you wrong.

CHAPTER TEN

1. kindness
2. joy
3. love
4. service
5. caring
6. sharing
7. wisdom
8. understanding
9. forgiveness
10. hope
11. humility
12. confession
13. honor
14. goodness
15. peace

Series for Young Readers*
From Bethany House Publishers

★ ★ ★

THE ADVENTURES OF CALLIE ANN
by Shannon Mason Leppard

Readers will giggle their way through the true-to-life escapades of Callie Ann Davies and her many North Carolina friends.

★ ★ ★

BACKPACK MYSTERIES
by Mary Carpenter Reid

This excitement-filled mystery series follows the mishaps and adventures of Steff and Paulie Larson as they strive to help often-eccentric relatives crack their toughest cases.

★ ★ ★

THE CUL-DE-SAC KIDS
by Beverly Lewis

Each story in this lighthearted series features the hilarious antics and predicaments of nine endearing boys and girls who live on Blossom Hill Lane.

★ ★ ★

RUBY SLIPPERS SCHOOL
by Stacy Towle Morgan

Join the fun as home-schoolers Hope and Annie Brown visit fascinating countries and meet inspiring Christians from around the world!

★ ★ ★

THREE COUSINS DETECTIVE CLUB®
by Elspeth Campbell Murphy

Famous detective cousins Timothy, Titus, and Sarah-Jane learn compelling Scripture-based truths while finding—and solving—intriguing mysteries.

* (ages 7–10)

9611